# DOCTOR DEATH

Edgar J. Hyde

Published in 2009
by Igloo Books Ltd
Cottage Farm
Sywell
NN6 0BJ

www.igloo-books.com

10 9 8 7 6 5 4 3 2 1

ISBN: 978-1-84817-520-4
Printed and manufactured in China

# Contents

# Chapter 1:

# Sporting Heroes

Ever gone to visit the doctor but felt worse afterwards instead of better? Well, that's just what happened to Josh Stevens and a few of his best buddies when *Dr Death*, as he quickly became known, came to practice in their town. Let me tell you what happened . . .

"Go, Josh!" Simon yelled to his best friend as he passed him, changing pace slightly, to bounce the ball in Josh's direction. Josh caught the ball as it bounced back up, ducking out of the way of the Merton Vale defence. He jumped, aiming straight for the basketball net. Almost in slow motion, as everyone in the gym sucked in their breath, the ball gently circled the rim of the net. Josh could see, from the corner of his eye, Coach Barnes get up from the bench and stand, staring at the ball, almost willing it to drop through the net. It worked, or at least something did, for the next minute it seemed as though the entire school erupted as the ball finally stopped circling and fell straight through the basket.

# Creepers

They had won. Their team had beaten Merton Vale for the first time in seven years and Josh had scored the winning basket. Simon and the rest of the team whooped gloriously, punching the air in delighted victory, everyone grinning from ear to ear.

"Brilliant, Josh, just brilliant." Coach Barnes slapped Josh on the back. "Had us on the edge of our seats there, though. Thought the final whistle was going to blow before you scored. Well done, Josh, well done!"

As the losing team left to commiserate with each other in the shower room, the boys revelled in their victory. Everyone in the gym remained standing, applauding the first team to bring back the cup in so many years. Grabbed from behind, Josh was hoisted aloft on his team-mates' shoulders. They carried him on their lap of honor singing "For he's a jolly good fellow" at the tops of their voices – and Josh loved it. Every minute of it. He had never felt so special in all his life, and he was determined to savour every moment. He played to the crowd, waving and smiling to them, not caring that his hair was stuck to his head, his face scarlet and dripping with perspiration. As they began on their second lap of honor, Josh noticed Karen with some of her friends. Karen Summers, the love of his life – and she had just witnessed his moment of glory, his five minutes of fame. Josh gave her a special smile as he passed by. She just *had* to go out with him now. How could she refuse to go out with the High School hero? All Josh had to do was pluck up the courage and ask her, and he'd have a date for Saturday night with the best looking-girl in school. The team stopped at the far end of the pitch and the boys lowered Josh to the ground. Still euphoric, but calmer now, they stood proudly alongside the Coach while the Headmaster, Mr Jenkins, pinned on their winners' medals.

"Well done, son," he congratulated Josh. "It's a proud day for us all."

He moved on to the next boy in line and Josh glanced up at Coach Barnes. He winked at Josh and nodded his head slowly, in the way someone does when they're glad about what you've just done. Josh smiled back, straightened his shoulders and puffed out his chest with pride. He wanted the moment to go on and on forever.

Later, in the showers, there was lots of fooling around as they all good naturedly splashed one another. Smelly tee-shirts, shorts and sneakers thrown into sports bags, the friends walked out of the school gates and started to make their way home. Every second of the game was dissected, discussed and looked at from every angle. Every goal they'd scored was exaggerated, with players jumping higher, dribbling faster and scoring much easier than any other team they'd ever seen. In conclusion – though this was far from the truth, for the other team was a more than worthy opponent – the boys decided their rivals needn't have been there at all, so great were the circles they had run around them.

As the boys neared home, so the animated little band grew smaller.

"Bye Kev – see you tomorrow," shouted Simon as Kevin left them to cross the road to his house. In answer, Kevin raised his arm in a victory salute and ran happily up his front pathway.

"See you guys," said Charlie, bending to tie his shoelace.

"See you, Charlie," Josh returned as he and Simon continued their walk.

"Did you see Karen Summers?" Josh asked as he turned to look at his best friend.

"I sure did," Simon replied.

"How could I miss her? She was the one who cheered loudest when you scored the winner."

"She was?" Josh asked, looking at his friend to see whether or not he was joking, but his face remained impassive.

"Look, Josh..." He stopped and turned to face him. "You've got to ask the girl for a date. I mean, everyone knows you're mad about her, everyone except her that is. I'm telling you, if you don't move quickly someone else is going to snap her up from right under your nose. That girl's too pretty by far to be left on her own for any length of time."

"I know, Simon," Josh sighed. "But what if she says no?"

Having just resumed walking, Simon stopped again. "Josh, man, are you kidding me? Look, how many times have we gone over this – you're an okay guy, Josh, I never saw any reason before why she shouldn't go out with you, but now, after today?" In a rare show of affection, or perhaps it was sheer exasperation, Simon punched his friend on the shoulder. "Go for it kid," he smiled. "Hey, what's the worst thing that can happen?"

Josh smiled back, wishing he felt as confident as Simon looked. They had stopped just outside Josh's gate. He undid the latch and said goodbye to his friend. "Thanks, Si, see you tomorrow. And remember, Thornton High is the best." They gave each other a "high five" and Josh pushed open his front door.

# Chapter 2:

# A Spot of Bother

"It's me, Mom," he shouted, dropping his sports bag in the hall. "Guess what?" he went on as he headed for the kitchen. "We won the cup – first time in seven years – and guess who scored the winning goal?"

He heard mom start to come down the stairs as he took a can of Coke from the fridge.

"Josh – is that you?" she began.

"I hope you haven't left dirty sports kit in your bag – put it in the washing machine if you want it washed. You kids seem to think clean clothes appear magically in your drawers, having spent a couple of days lying on the floor. Never seem to think of washing machines, tumble dryers and irons, do you?"

Josh took a bite from a Snickers bar and didn't bother to answer. He didn't need to – his mother answered all her own questions anyway. Carrying the offending sports bag, his mom entered the kitchen.

"What's this, then?" she asked, waving the bag around in front of Josh's face.

"Dirty sports kit, that's what."

See – the mother who answered all her own questions! Josh turned to look at his mom, vaguely curious to know if he would be allowed to answer anything she asked him today.

"And what's that you're eating? Chocolate! You'll never be able to eat dinner, Josh. I don't know why you have to snack between meals. Don't they give you enough to eat at school? Oh, I know, don't tell me, you didn't fancy what was on the menu so you and Simon went to the baker's and had a snack."

She actually looked at her son at that point for confirmation. Unfortunately, Josh had too much chocolate in his mouth to answer in the positive or negative, so he just had to let her carry on. Filling up the little plastic ball with washing powder, she turned the dial on the washing machine and clicked the switch to 'on'. Straightening up, she spotted the half empty Coke in Josh's hand.

"Josh!" she admonished. "When will you ever learn? Chocolate *and* fizzy drinks! Your spots will never clear up if you don't stop eating so much junk food."

"I know, Mom," Josh said, draining what was

left of the Coke. "But somehow a piece of fruit and a glass of water just don't hold the same attraction, you know?"

The washing machine had started its cycle and Josh walked upstairs to change out of his school clothes. "I wonder why that little plastic ball never melts?" he wondered as he reached the top of the stairs.

"Josh," Mom shouted after him. "Did you hear what I said? I'm taking you to see our new doctor tomorrow – Dr Blair, I think his name is – to see if he can do anything to help your skin. I'll pick you up straight after school, okay? And don't, for Heaven's sake, tell him you pig out on candy bars and cans of Coke. Let me do the talking, if you don't mind."

"Let *me* do the talking," Josh thought to himself. Just who was she kidding? With his mother around no-one else ever got the chance to do *any* talking, least of all him. He flopped on top of his bed and stretched over to reach the little hand mirror on his bedside table. His spots were a lot better, he thought, as he examined himself in the mirror. Sure, his forehead could look quite bad, but if he just kept his hair that little bit longer, and remembered to brush it in a certain way, it practically covered his spots over. Still, it wouldn't do any harm to see this new guy – maybe he could come up with something old Dr Feldman hadn't known about. The old man had retired from practice, a lot later than he should have according to his mum, and this new guy must be the one who had taken his place.

"Dr Blair, eh?" he thought to himself. "Well, then, let's see if you know your stuff."

# Chapter 3:

# Doctor Popular

Next day Charlie wasn't at school.

"His mom said he had a – now, how was it she put it?" Kevin laughed.

"Oh yes, an 'upset tummy'" he finished, doing a passable imitation of Charlie's mom's voice.

"When I called for him this morning that's what she said.

Not 'Sorry, Kev, he can't get off the toilet seat', or 'Sorry, Kev, he has a runny bottom', just 'Sorry, Kev, he has an upset tummy – too much excitement yesterday probably'."

Josh and Simon laughed too, thinking of all the fun they'd have when Charlie got back to school, making loud wind noises in class, putting toilet rolls in his school bag, and so on.

Josh sat on his own during his geography period, as it was the absent Charlie who normally sat beside him in this class. He didn't mind one bit, though, for he spent the whole of the class staring at the back of Karen Summers' head. He had chosen this seat specially at the start of term. It was the only class he shared with Karen and he had been determined he should sit close by her for at least half an hour twice a week. As the bell rang to signify the end of the period, she stood up to gather her books. She turned to Josh.

"Congratulations, Josh. You played brilliantly yesterday – you must be really proud."

She smiled, and waited to see what Josh would say.

"Gee, thanks," he muttered, rising to his feet.

He tugged at his hair self-consciously, pulling it forward to hide the horrible spots on his forehead. As he stood up, he knocked over his chair, which in turn knocked over the chair behind him, then knocked against the desk.

"Sorry, sorry," he stammered, blushing furiously and turning to help whoever he'd knocked over behind him.

The desk and chair were empty, a fact he'd been well aware of earlier, but had forgotten in his embarrassment. Righting both desk and chair, he coughed to cover his unease and turned back to Karen, trying desperately to think of something smart and funny to say. She'd gone.

He was practically the last one left in the

classroom, apart from that pathetic little teacher's pet Jones, who was always at the front of the class, asking the teachers one thing or another. Karen, beautiful, perfect Karen, had gone.

Sighing heavily, he picked up his books and left the classroom. He could kick himself. What an idiot! The chance of a lifetime and he'd blown it. He'd better not tell Simon, or he'd go crazy – and after all wasn't he entitled to? Friday afternoon – second last period – and he blew what could have been his first Saturday night date with Karen. He had no idea what his history teacher spoke about for the next period as he remonstrated with himself over and over again.

Finally, after what seemed an age, the bell rang and he was able to leave school. As he came through the outer doors, he was surprised to see his mother's car parked outside. She tooted noisily and signaled to him to hurry up. He'd forgotten. The doctor's appointment.

Though he may as well be covered in spots from head to toe considering the way he'd just behaved with Karen.

Great huge boils, he thought, as he crossed the road. With a few white heads and some large green ones oozing with pus, just for good measure. Whole face may as well be one huge spot, for that matter, with green *and* yellow poison seeping from it.

"Hi, Mom," he said as he opened the car door. Checking her mirror and putting the car into gear, Mrs Stevens pulled away.

"Hi yourself," she smiled. "And what's made you so unhappy on this fine day?"

Josh shrugged and looked out of the window.

"I was talking to Charlie's mom today. You didn't tell me your team won the basketball trophy yesterday, or that you scored the winning goal?"

"I did, Mom" Josh began. "You just weren't listening..."

"I said to Marjorie this morning, now isn't that just typical of my son. Never tells me anything that may be important – spends all his time out of school holed up in his room, making occasional foraging visits to the fridge. Marjorie said herself she probably wouldn't have known either, only Charlie wasn't himself last night, an upset tummy she said, and apparently that's how he gets when he's been over-excited. She said you all got medals and that it was the first time you had won the cup in – how many years? Oh yes, seven, that's right."

Josh raised his eyes heavenwards then resumed looking out of the window. He wondered briefly if

# Doctor Death

Karen was capable of droning on like this. Horrified, he shut the thought out very quickly. No, he decided, this trait was exclusive to his mother, surely, this was simply his mom being his mom.

Arriving at the surgery, neither Josh nor his mom could believe their eyes. The car park was filled to capacity, and there were cars double parked on either side of the road.

"Good Heavens," Mrs Stevens breathed as she circled the car park for the third time, "there must be some sort of epidemic. I've never seen the surgery so busy in all my life."

Josh had to agree – even the annual summer event held in the school grounds didn't attract as many people as this. He wondered what on earth was going on.

"Look mom – over there," he pointed.

"Oh yes, dear, well spotted." Mrs Winterman from the bakery had just come out of the surgery and was getting ready to reverse her car out of the car park. "I wonder what's wrong with her?" Mrs Stevens thought aloud.

"She doesn't *look* ill, I have to say."

Josh and his mom were dumbfounded when they pushed open the door of the surgery. There wasn't a seat to be had in the place.

# Creepers

Mothers with toddlers squirming on their laps were seated next to young girls with new babies, who in turn sat beside elderly arthritic ladies who clutched their walking sticks to their sides.

The normally composed receptionist was rushed off her feet, the phone was ringing off the hook, buzzers buzzing and people continuously demanded appointments. As Mrs Stevens and Josh approached the desk the receptionist was finishing a call.

"Yes, that's fine, Mrs Collins, two weeks on Monday at 9.30am." She searched frantically for her pen. Josh pointed to behind his ear and she looked at him quizzically. She lifted the appointments book and looked underneath that before checking in her pocket. Josh again tapped the side of his head, just above his ear.

"Sorry, Mrs Collins, just a moment – I seem to have mislaid my pen."

She touched her hand to the side of her head and at once located the missing object. Smiling her thanks to Josh, she wrote in the appointment, said goodbye to her caller and replaced the handset. Pushing her hair back from her eyes, she looked expectantly at Mrs Stevens.

"Oh . . . Josh Stevens," said his mom. "We have an appointment with Dr Blair at 4.30."

# Doctor Death

The buzzer buzzed. The receptionist checked her book then leaned forward to shout through the glass partition.

"Mrs Burns, Dr Blair will see you now." She watched Mrs Burns make her way into the doctor's room then turned back towards Josh.

"I'm afraid we're running a little behind schedule. We've just been so busy, as I'm sure you can see – but if you'd like to take a seat, if you can find one, that is – I'm sure the doctor shouldn't be too long."

Josh was about to say they'd come back some other day, but his mother obviously fancied sitting there for hours and hours reading out-of-date magazines because she merely smiled, thanked the receptionist and went off in search of a seat.

Josh had never been so bored in his whole life. He'd spent the first 15 minutes of his wait trying not to breathe the same air as the twins who sat on his right-hand side. They looked as if they had a bad case of chickenpox, and Josh certainly didn't want to be afflicted with that. He had more than enough spots to contend with.

After that, he tried to work out on average whether he'd eaten more Snickers or Hershey Bars this week. (He was learning all about averages in his math class just now, and tended to practice the theory on just about everything, including how many visits he paid to the bathroom in a period of one week.) It was no use, though, he couldn't remember whether he'd had a Hershey on Wednesday or if that had been the day he'd deviated and had a Milky Way.

He glanced at his mom and wondered if it was worthwhile suggesting they leave. She was chewing her left thumbnail, the way she always did when she was concentrating on something. Leaning closer, Josh was able to see she was immersed in an article entitled *"Does your Partner Really Listen?"* No point in suggesting leaving then. He sighed, shifting uncomfortably in his seat.

It was getting hot in here now, too. He pulled at the neck of his sweatshirt. He'd have to take his jacket off soon.

"Don't fidget, Josh," his mom said absent mindedly, never taking her eyes from her magazine.

"Mrs Stevens," called the red-faced, harassed receptionist.

"Mrs Stevens, Dr Blair will see you now."

"Oh, right." His mom sat up with a jolt, her front teeth going right through her thumbnail as she did so.

"Damn," she murmured involuntarily then,

straightening her skirt, she smiled apologetically at the waiting patients as she pushed past and, with Josh following  just behind, she entered Dr Blair's room.

# Chapter 4:

# Doctor Perfect

"Mrs Stevens, how nice to meet you." Dr Blair got up and walked towards them, his hand outstretched towards Josh's mom. "And you must be Josh," he smiled at the boy, still holding onto Mrs Stevens' hand. Josh looked at his mother, noting that she didn't seem to be trying too hard to disentangle herself from the doctor's grasp.

"Please, take a seat," the doctor continued, as he finally let go of Mrs Steven's hand and closed the door.

Barbara Stevens was flabberghasted. Now she knew why the waiting room was crammed full of females. This guy was drop-dead gorgeous! At least 6 feet 2, a shock of unruly dark hair, and the most piercing blue eyes she'd ever had the pleasure of looking into.

Josh nudged her sharply with his elbow.

"What? Oh, sorry, Dr Blair – did you ask me something?"

Shifting in her seat, Mrs Stevens cleared her throat

and tried to concentrate on what the doctor was saying, instead of staring into his deep blue eyes.

Dr Blair smiled, a slow lazy smile that lit up his whole face. Eyes twinkling, he picked up his pen before opening Josh's file.

"What exactly can I help you with today?" he repeated, looking from Mrs Stevens to Josh, then back again to Mrs Stevens.

Gathering her composure, Mrs Stevens leaned over Josh and pushed his hair back from his face.

"It's his skin, Dr Blair. Spots, you see, lots of them."

"There aren't that many, Mom" Josh flushed, embarrassed. Ignoring him, Mom went on. "They can get a lot worse than this, and sometimes his whole face is affected. I just wondered if there was any cream you would recommend he should use, other than the one he has at present. He can be a bit sensitive, you know, at his age, starting to get interested in girls, though he pretends otherwise, don't you Josh?"

She smiled and winked at Josh, as though they shared some sort of special secret. That was it. The ultimate embarrassment. Josh wanted to die. First of all his mother going all silly over the new doctor, then having to sit there while she exposed all his spots, and now telling this stranger that he was into girls! Josh flushed to his roots, knowing as he did so that it only made his spots stand out all the more, red angry pimples all clustered together on his forehead.

Dr Blair got up and came over for a closer look, though Josh thought he could have seen perfectly well from the other side of his desk, so big did he think his spots now appeared. He bent and peered closely at the mortified boy's forehead.

"Ah, yes," he mumbled. "Just a mild form of acne. Nothing we can't deal with here."

Acne! thought Josh. Acne! Old Doc Feldman hadn't said it was acne. Just some teenage spots, he'd said. Not acne! How terrible. He couldn't tell his pals about this. What if Karen got to find out? She'd never go out with a boy with acne, school basketball hero or not! He'd have to keep this *very* quiet.

He turned to hear what the doctor was saying, at the same time making himself a silent promise never to snack on chocolate and fizzy drinks ever again.

"No need go to the pharmacy – I have some ointment already made up here, Mrs Stevens," Dr Blair was saying. He took a small tub of clear ointment from his drawer and placed it on the desk in front of him.

"There you go, Josh. Simply rub that into the spots

every night before you go to bed and you'll soon see a marked difference, I can promise you."

Mrs Stevens lifted the tub and put it into her handbag. "Thank you ever so much, Dr Blair, you've been very kind. Should we make another appointment to come back and see you – you know, just to see how he's progressing?"

She put her head on one side as she stood up, and her voice sounded silly and squeaky as she spoke. Josh wanted to be sick. His mother *fancied* the doctor! She was a complete embarrassment. She always did the "head-on-one-side-squeaky-voice bit" when she liked someone. He'd seen it all before and each time it made him cringe.

"There shouldn't be any need, I don't think," replied the doctor. "But if you feel another visit's necessary then, yes, I should be delighted to see you."

He opened the door and again shook Mrs Stevens' hand.

"It's been a real pleasure," he told her. "See you again some time."

"Thank you, Dr Blair, thank you," mom gushed as she almost tripped over a toy lying on the waiting room floor. Regaining her balance, she smiled her thanks once more and made to leave.

# Doctor Death

"Anyone would think he'd just performed life -saving open-heart surgery on me the way she's going on," Josh thought to himself as he too left the room.

"Spots, Josh?" The doctor spoke softly. Josh turned back to look at him. "You ain't seen nothin' yet."

Then, pressing his buzzer, he asked for his next patient to be sent in.

"What did you just say?" asked Josh, who thought he must be hearing things.

His face like stone now, the twinkly smile long gone, Dr Blair glanced briefly at the boy.

"Close the door, I said. You're causing a draught."

# Chapter 5:

# Spot the Difference

Josh threw an apple core into the bin. He'd resolved firmly in his mind that he was turning over a new leaf. No more junk food, and an ointment application every night. He was determined to rid himself once and for all of his spots, *and* determined not to pay another visit to Dr Blair's surgery ever again. Today had been the ultimate humiliation for him, and if his mother wanted to see the good doctor again, she could go on her own.

Josh certainly wouldn't be accompanying her, that was for sure. And that closing remark, now that *was* strange. Josh didn't know whether he was imagining things or not but, even if he had imagined what the doctor's parting words were, he certainly hadn't imagined the look on his face.

"A complete change from when Mom was around," the boy thought as he unscrewed the lid of the tub and dipped his finger into the ointment. "Here goes, then," he told his reflection as he began rubbing the cream onto his forehead. "Over to you,

# Creepers

Dr Blair – do your worst!"

Reaching out of bed next morning, he shut out Bart Simpson's voice on his alarm clock. He yawned sleepily and snuggled back under the covers.

"Just another ten minutes," he thought, as he did every morning, knowing full well that his mom would wake him if he didn't appear for breakfast on time.

Cocooned like a caterpillar in his quilt, he allowed himself to wake slowly, letting thoughts of what today would bring creep into his head.

"Saturday," he thought happily.

"Paper round, back for a huge breakfast then meet Simon and the rest of the gang for some serious hanging about down at the mall. Might even spot Karen down there, if I'm lucky. Spot!" he thought, suddenly alert. "I'd forgotten the spot cream. I wonder if it's worked yet." Jumping out of bed with a crash, and causing his mother to tut from her position at the breakfast table downstairs, he rushed over to his dressing table mirror for a look.

He gasped. "Holy cow – what the – I can't believe this. No, no!" he shouted.

"Mom, come up here, you have to help me. Mom, come quickly, please."

Babs Stevens took the stairs two at a time. He

must have fallen when she heard the crash, and she thought he'd just been mucking about as usual.

Dear Lord, he'd probably cracked his head open on the bedside table.

"Josh," she flew into the room. "What is it, baby, what's wrong?" She stopped in her tracks. The boy was fine, kneeling in front of his dressing table mirror with not a scratch in sight.

"Josh Stevens," she admonished, sitting on the edge of his bed to catch her breath. "You gave me such a fright – I thought there was something wrong, that you'd fallen and hurt yourself."

"Wrong! Wrong! Of course there's something wrong – look at my face, or what's left of my face. You know the expression 'Can't see the wood for the trees?', well try 'Can't see the face for the spots!'"

Mrs Stevens looked more closely at her son. "Oh, yes," she agreed. "I see what you mean. There *are* a few more this morning. And what's that one on the bridge of your nose – is it green or yellow pus?"

She bent forward to touch Josh's face and he pulled away quickly.

"Don't touch them, Mom, you'll spread them even further." He turned back to the mirror, horrified.

"A few more!" Well, if that wasn't the understatement of the century. Yesterday's cluster of red pimples had now multiplied, and it wasn't just his forehead that was affected. He had a sprinkling on either cheek, the offending one on the bridge of his nose, and the ones that had always been on his forehead had doubled in size and filled up with alternating pockets of green or yellow pus. He simply couldn't believe his eyes.

"I can't go out looking like this, mom. Young children will take fright, cats and dogs will take to their heels in terror, my friends won't want to be seen with me, and what if I see Karen?"

Horrified at the prospect of coming face to face with the girl he had eagerly looked forward to seeing just a few minutes earlier, Josh shook his head in dismay. His mother reached out to pat his shoulder comfortingly.

"Josh, Josh, calm down, come on now. It's not as bad as you think. Once you've washed your hair and dried it over your forehead the way you usually do, you won't look half so bad, honestly."

"It's that new cream," Josh said disgustedly.

"I should never have listened to you and that new doctor. My skin wasn't so bad yesterday, and look at me now – I look as though I just spent four hours in make-up getting ready for a part in a Freddie Krueger movie!"

# Doctor Death

Mrs Stevens suppressed a smile and picked up the tub of cream.

"Listen, Josh," she said softly. "It says here on the side of the tub 'may make condition worse before any improvement is seen'. You see – worse before it gets better. Your Gran used to say that, don't you remember?"

"Sure, I remember," Josh said huffily, "only I thought it was just another old wives' tale."

"Well, there may be some truth in this one," said mom as she replaced the tub on the dressing table. "Look, Josh, try and see the positive side of this. It's Saturday, right? You apply the cream tonight again and then you'll have the whole day Sunday to mope about the house looking spotty and feeling horrible. Then you apply the cream on Sunday night and, hey presto, Monday morning you get up for school with the clearest, most spot-free skin in the world. So you have the worst days at home at the weekend and the better days back at school with your friends where it really matters."

Josh looked at her hopefully. "You really think so, Mom?" You think that's what'll happen?"

"Well, it's possible, isn't it?" his mother answered, hiding her crossed fingers behind her back. "Come on, let's go, you've got a paper round to do. And no buts!" She put her fingers to her son's lips, stopping his protests.

"You do *not* look nearly as bad as you think, Josh, and half the world's still asleep anyway."

"Go on, go and get showered and off you go. I'll have a huge breakfast waiting for you when you get back, so go work up an appetite!"

Josh turned on the shower tap and started to hum a little tune. Mom was right. He had all weekend to get rid of the spots, and the prospect of being rid of them completely was almost too staggering for words.

Maybe he should apply the cream more often than just once at night. Yes, that's what he'd do – he'd apply it once every few hours just to speed the process along. He let the hot water run over his hair and down his back. Gee, he could hardly wait till Monday morning.

Arriving at the mall later that day, Josh was both surprised and pleased to see Charlie there with Kevin and Simon.

"Hey, Charlie" he called. "Howya doin?"

Charlie turned towards his friend and smiled weakly.

"Gosh, you look awful" said Josh, aghast.

And he did, too. His face looked thinner,

somehow – his eyes seeming to sink deep into their sockets – and his pallor was distinctly on the gray side.

"Thanks, Josh, you sure know how to make a guy feel better!"

"Sorry," said Josh. "I didn't mean to... it's just that you normally look..."

Charlie held up his hand to quieten his friend. "It's okay, Josh, really, it's cool. I know how I look. I don't feel that great, either, I have to admit. But don't tell my mom I said that – I had a hard enough job persuading her to let me come out today as it was."

Josh and the others nodded sympathetically. They knew what their own mothers were like, after all.

"Anyway," Charlie continued, "yesterday was awful. In fact, I got so bad Mom bundled me into the car last night and took me over to see the doctor – the new guy, you know, Dr Blair? So, he checks me over and gives me some sachets of stuff I have to drink three times a day. Says that should sort me out. Strangely enough, though, I've had two sachets today already and I can honestly say that I'm actually feeling worse!"

"Now that is weird," began Josh.

"Cos I saw Dr Blair yesterday, too. Strange guy, I thought, couldn't make my mind up whether or not

I liked him, though my mom didn't seem to have the same problem."

"Oh, not yours too!" said Charlie. "I wanted to *vomit* in the nearest bucket the way my mother was carrying on. Fluffing up her hair, and pretending to be a young thing, real squirm-in-your-seat stuff."

"I know exactly what you mean," said Josh in agreement. "Sort of behavior you'd expect from a teenager. So, anyway, this Dr Blair, he gave me some ointment to put on my spots and told me to apply it every night. Thing was, that when I woke up this morning... " He broke off.

"Charlie – you okay?"

"I'm fine, Josh," Charlie managed to say through clenched teeth, his face contorting with pain. "I just have to get to the bathroom, that's all. I'll be okay."

Clutching his stomach, Charlie started to move away in the direction of the escalator that would take him to the bathrooms located on the lower level. Unfortunately, the guys were treated to the unwelcome stench of some gas that had escaped before Charlie moved away.

"Oh man," said Kevin, holding his nose dramatically. "Let's get out of here."

Some loud noises were emanating from Charlie's direction, too, as he tried to hurry to the escalator.

## Doctor Death

"We'll meet you in the Do-nut Diner," shouted Simon as the three moved away. Turning to Josh, Simon added, "though maybe your mom was right about you staying away from sugar, Josh. Your face does look a bit of a mess today."

"Thanks, Si, I can always rely on you to boost my confidence just when I really need it!"

# Chapter 6:

# A Turn for the Worse

On Monday morning when Simon arrived at Josh's house, Josh stuck his head firmly under the covers and refused to come downstairs.

"He's still in bed, Simon," said Mrs Stevens. "Go up and see him if you like."

"Thanks, Mrs Stevens, I will," said Simon, brushing past her to go upstairs. Mrs Stevens stepped back against the wall. What on earth was that smell?

"Simon, have you trod in dog's dirt? Let me check your shoes."

Simon stopped and showed the soles of both shoes. Clean. Turning his face away, he muttered, "It's not my shoes, Mrs Stevens, I only wish it was."

There it was again, that same smell. Maybe it was coming from outside. She opened the door wider to go and check and Simon took the opportunity to climb the stairs to Josh's room. Josh was still under the covers when his friend came in.

"Go away, Simon. I'm going nowhere today, or

for the rest of my life for that matter. I *really* look like something out of a horror movie now."

Simon sat on the bed beside his friend.

"I know just what you mean, Josh – and believe me, the best place you could be right now is underneath the covers and away from the smell of my breath!"

This statement caused Josh to move slightly, though not enough for him to stick his head out from his hiding place. His voice was muffled.

"What do you mean, Simon? What smell?"

"If I mentioned the name of Dr Blair to you, you might understand what I'm about to tell you."

More movement from under the covers.

"My mom was going to the doctor's Saturday evening and I went with her, mostly out of curiosity after what you and Charlie said about him. And you were right. Mr Perfect, in Mom's eyes anyway. She thought he was totally gorgeous and I think, judging by the number of females in the waiting room, that so do half the population of the town. Anyway – he deals with Mom's problem then turns his attention to me. 'And what about you, young man – are you in perfect health, or is there anything I can help you with?' he says. So, just as I'm about to tell him fine, Mom butts in and tells him about the verruca on my foot. I mean, I've had the thing for ages, I'm treating it myself with verruca ointment and there simply isn't a problem. Between you and me, though, I think Mom just wanted to prolong the visit and spend as much time as she could drooling over this guy.

When I tell him what I've been treating my foot with, he says he has a better cure and gives me a small bottle of pills. 'Take two of these a day,' he tells me, 'and before you know it your problem will be solved.' So I did – Saturday and Sunday. Then last night I started to notice it – the smell I mean." He sighed wearily. "Josh, come on, take your head out of the covers. I promise I won't laugh. I've got serious problems of my own, believe me."

Slowly, Josh sat up in his bed, revealing a face now almost completely covered in huge red, yellow and green spots. Simon let out a long low whistle.

"Wow, man, he sure did a good job on you."

Josh dived straight back under the covers.

"Hey, Simon, you weren't kidding about the smell. Can you open my window, please?"

Offended, though understanding Josh's request totally, Simon opened the window as far as it would go.

"Okay, Josh, it's open, I'll breathe out this way if you want to come out again."

# Creepers

Josh popped his head back out of the covers.

"Go on, then," he prompted, "and explain the remark 'sure did a good job on you'. What exactly do you mean?"

"Dr Blair, Josh, that's who I mean. Don't ask me why, 'cos I don't have an explanation, but this guy's out to get us. You, me, Charlie – look at us. Each one afflicted with something awful and embarrassing immediately following a visit to his surgery. My breath is so foul it's almost as though he's transferred the smell of my feet after being stuck in my sneakers through a whole basketball game into my mouth. Your mom thought I'd trod in something when I came in, it's so bad."

Josh couldn't dispute that. Despite his window being opened fully, he was glad when his friend stopped talking and therefore spreading the foul smell of his breath around the room. He was grateful too soon.

"And another thing," Simon continued. "I met the teachers pet Jones on my way over here and he was positively reeking of BO. Now a pain he may be, but he never suffered from BO before. *And* I saw him in Dr Blair's surgery on Saturday night, so if that doesn't tell you something then what does!"

Josh shook his head in disbelief.

# Doctor Death

"But why, Simon? Why would a doctor want to *give* people ailments, instead of trying to cure them?"

Simon shrugged. "I don't know, Josh, it doesn't make any sense to me either. What I do know though is that our Dr Blair isn't the nice gentlemanly type he would have our mothers believe. While they're swooning all over the place, Dr Blair here's handing out all sorts of weird potions that cause more grief than you'd care to believe. *And* he tried to shut my fingers in the door as I was leaving, only I was too quick for him."

Josh looked at his friend doubtfully. "Come on, Si, that's a bit childish, isn't it? A doctor trying to shut your fingers in a door?"

"I know how it sounds, Josh," said Simon, forgetting to breathe out of the window, and causing Josh to reel back against his headboard, "but I'm telling you he did. And the look on his face when I managed to get out of the way in time was not one of pleasure, I can tell you."

Josh remembered the doctor's parting words to him on his visit to the surgery, when he thought he'd merely misheard. He repeated the words to Simon.

"'Spots – you ain't seen nothin' yet.' And, boy, was he ever right!" said Josh, snatching a quick glance at himself in the mirror. The two boys sat in silence for a few minutes, each with his own thoughts.

"Tell you what," said Josh eventually. "Mom's determined I should go to school today – who's she kidding – so let's behave as though we are going to school but go visit Dr Blair, and see if we can find out just what he's up to. I'll just grab a quick shower and we'll go."

Just as he got out of bed, his bedroom door opened and Charlie and Kevin entered. Charlie was whiter than ever and sat down very gingerly on the bed. His many visits to the bathroom had caused his nether regions to become somewhat "inflamed", as his mother put it. "Red raw" was closer to how Charlie would have described it.

"What's the weird smell in here?" He looked at Josh. "And it's not me – I've only just arrived."

Simon turned from the window. "I'm afraid it's me guys, and I'm afraid you're gonna have to put up with it until we can all find cures for our ailments."

"I'm just going into the shower," said Josh as he made to leave the room.

"I'll leave Simon to fill you guys in on what we've been discussing." As he pushed past Kevin he stopped for a closer look. "What's that on the end of your nose, Kev, a wart?"

# Doctor Death

Self-consciously touching the new growth at the end of his nose, Kevin nodded.

"Hay fever," he said. "That was all I went to him for – some hay fever tablets – and now look at me!"

# Chapter 7:

# Hatching a Plan

The four boys made their way to the local park, taking a long detour around the school, hoping not to be spotted by any teachers, or parents for that matter. The park keeper didn't seem to be about so they headed for the maze. Having frequented the maze for years, each of them knew exactly which way to go, and they also knew they'd be fairly safe at the centre of the maze from any unwelcome prying eyes. They sat cross-legged, Charlie grimacing as he sat down beside his friends. Where before the others would have laughed at their friend's misfortune, having now been afflicted themselves they were a bit more sympathetic.

"Okay, guys," Josh began. "We have to form a plan to find out just what the good doctor's up to. And to rid ourselves of these ailments. I mean, look at us – a more motley crew you've never set eyes on. Although you look all right, Simon, you'd be fine if you could learn sign language and keep your mouth shut for the rest of your life."

Simon managed a wry smile. "Yeah, right, Josh. I know how bad it is. And I want it sorted out. We have to find out what this guy's up to, what sort of medicinal concoction he's given each of us, and if there's any way of reversing the process."

The boys nodded in agreement.

"Okay," said Kevin,

"Here's what I think we should do. There's no point in going to the surgery just now – you know how busy it is every day. We really need to go there when the clinic's over, sneak in somehow and see exactly what's what."

"You're right," agreed Charlie. "We'll have to go later tonight when things are a bit quieter. I want to get Dr Blair back for what he's done – make him pay for all this suffering.

"That's what we'll do then," said Simon, "only if we're going to stay here all day we'll need some provisions – we're bound to get hungry."

"I'll go" said Charlie, getting to his feet. "I have to go to the bathroom anyway, so I'll go to the shops when I'm out and buy some chips and juice and stuff."

The boys emptied their pockets and gave Charlie what money they had.

"I hate to tell you, Kev," he said as he turned to

leave, "but I think you just grew another wart on your chin!"

So having spent the day in the maze, with poor Charlie making frequent trips in and out to the bathroom (and reporting sightings of children he knew sporting huge cauliflower ears they had not previously had), the four boys all dropped their school bags back home, pretending to their mothers they'd had perfectly normal days in school. They met up again at the top of the road leading to the surgery and walked in silence towards Dr Blair's practice.

The flustered receptionist was just leaving, and about to lock the outer doors, when she saw the boys approach.

"Is the doctor still inside?" Josh asked anxiously.

"Yes, he's still there – though I don't think he'll be looking to see any more patients tonight. He's had a thoroughly exhausting day – as have I. Maybe you boys could come back tomorrow?"

Simon shrugged. "It's okay, nothing that can't wait. We'll come back another time, eh guys?" He winked conspiratorially at the others.

The receptionist smiled and finished locking the main doors.

"Bye then," she said, walking towards her car.

# Creepers

She unlocked the door, sat down and carefully checked the sole of each shoe. "Strange," she thought to herself. "There was a strong smell of dogs' dirt back then – could have sworn I'd trod in something."

"His surgery light's still on," said Kevin.

"He's probably planning even more horrors for any kids who call on him tomorrow. We've got to find a way in there."

Circling the building, the boys couldn't believe their luck when they discovered an open window.

"Quick!" said Josh. "Help me up. I'll go in and wait till he's gone, then I'll have a scout around and see if I can come up with anything. You lot stay here and see if you can find anything out from him when he leaves. Make sure he knows we're onto him – maybe if we back him into a corner he'll panic and do something stupid. The three friends, having watched Josh climb inside the surgery, walked about outside, chatting casually, kicking empty cans around, and generally trying to behave as normally as teenage boys do. They walked round to the front of the building and saw that the light was now out in Dr Blair's surgery. The three sauntered over to lean against his car, looking up casually as the doctor locked his surgery door.

# Doctor Death

"Get away from my car," he admonished them as soon as he saw them. "Troublemakers. Knew it the minute I set eyes on you."

Drawing closer to the boys, he grinned at Kevin, or at Kevin's warts.

"Working, I see," he said, obviously pleased. "And how's Charlie – still tied to the bathroom, my boy?" Reaching into his pocket for his car keys, he murmured almost to himself, "never lets me down, that one, always works a treat".

"So, you're admitting it, then?" asked Simon. "You did this to us deliberately. But why? Why would you want to do such a thing?"

"Oh," the doctor recoiled. "A bit too successful, that one," he said, covering his nose and taking a step backwards. "That really is the most foul-smelling breath I've come across in a long time. "Won't be very popular with anyone smelling like that, Simon, will you?"

Charlie pulled at his sleeve. "You've got to give us something to counteract these effects, doctor, please – can't you see how much we're suffering?"

Dr Blair disdainfully brushed Charlie's hand from his coat sleeve.

"How dare you touch me?" he hissed at the boy. "And don't tell me I *have* to help you! Why do you think I did this, after all? I enjoy seeing your suffering. Do you really think I'm going to spoil my fun and reverse the process? You can't be serious!"

"We'll tell our parents – we'll go to the police, expose you?" spluttered Kevin, enraged.

Dr Blair fixed his gaze on the boy.

"Kevin – ah yes, your mother was quite taken with me, if I remember correctly; as was yours, Simon, and yours, Charlie. Do you really think they'd believe I would do anything to harm their precious children, especially afflicting them with ailments as peculiar as these? I think not, brats, but take heart – the potions will wear off in a few years." He laughed, a cold chilling laugh that hung in the air.

Turning the key in the ignition, he rolled down the window.

"Believe me, boys, I'm living proof. I used to be ugly when I was a youth, covered in all manner of pimples and warts, but just look at me now! Females who wouldn't have spared me a glance when I was a teenager are now swooning all over my surgery. Eat your hearts out, guys." Taking his foot off the accelerator, he looked at each boy in turn. "Back off, boys, take this as a warning – I can get really nasty, and, believe me, you don't want to know about that.

# Doctor Death

If I were you I'd just be grateful I had only minor afflictions. They're not exactly life-threatening – yet!" He laughed again and pressed his foot to the floor.

"Life-threatening! Life-threatening! How dare he!" exploded Kevin.

"Calm down," said Simon, patting his friend's shoulder reassuringly. "We'll sort this whole thing out, don't you worry. But we have to stay calm and try to think straight. Come on, let's go see if Josh is okay – maybe he's found something that will help us."

The three boys went around to the open window, which, thankfully, the doctor had not noticed.

# Chapter 8:

# Kill or Cure?

Meanwhile Josh, inside, had indeed found "something". He had found jars and bottles bearing labels that claimed to do things which were beyond your wildest dreams.

After he jumped down from the window, he found himself in the small kitchen where the receptionist made her now infrequent cups of coffee and stealthily made his way to the surgery.

As there was still a fair bit of sunlight streaming through the window, he was able to see things quite clearly in the room. Everything seemed normal. The doctor's desk diary showed nothing untoward, though Josh did have a hard time deciphering some of the notes scribbled there.

"Typical doctor," he thought, then grinned wryly – this doctor was anything *but* typical!

The grey metal filing cabinets that lined the walls still had the keys in their locks. Josh opened the drawers easily. "Archer, Black, Dixon" – he read the names from the top drawer. Pushing that drawer back in, he pulled open the middle one. "M's and Macs seemed to take up most of the space in this one, so he moved on to the bottom. "Ramsay, Smith, Stevens – that's it." He pulled out his file. "Josh Stevens" it said on the front. Yeah, that was his address – it was definitely his file. Pulling up a chair beside the doctor's desk, he opened the file and started to read. "But it's all old stuff," he thought.

Like the time he had to have his knee stitched when he fell off his bike (his mom had insisted on removing his stabilisers, even though he had told her it was much too soon). And then the time he'd had an allergic reaction to a new brand of washing powder his mom had bought. Gee, that had been awful – covered in tiny little pin pricks from head to toe. He felt itchy just thinking about it! And look at that – he'd forgotten about that – the time he'd pushed one of his tiny green Lego bricks right up inside his nose and Doc Feldman had removed it with tweezers. Beginning to enjoy himself now, he leaned back in the chair and crossed his legs on the desk in front of him. He heard a noise.

"What was that?" he started, sitting upright at the desk. Then he noticed. What he'd earlier assumed to be simply a wall was in fact sliding doors, doors which had been covered perfectly in wallpaper to conceal behind them a huge walk-in closet. He must have inadvertently hit the button to open the doors when he put his feet on the table. He stood up and walked towards the now exposed closet.

Wow! The sight that greeted him was astounding. As he walked along the right hand side of the room (for it was far more fitting that it be called a room, being much too big to be known as a closet), he saw more jars, bottles, tubs and every other type of container than you could ever imagine. Glancing to his left, he saw it looked almost identical. They were both shelved. The jars on the top shelf were the largest, and were filled to capacity with different colored liquids. The containers on the second and third shelves were slightly smaller, and again filled with different colors of liquid. Concentrating on the left wall, then, Josh noticed that the bottom shelf held empty containers, in lots of different sizes, some of which were similar to the one his acne cream was in at home.

"So this is the doctor's dispensary," thought Josh, looking more closely at the jars, each of which was labelled very clearly and precisely. His eyes traveled along the top shelf. *Unbearable Itch* read the first label. *Hair Thinner* said the next. Followed by *Extremely Large and Flaky Dandruff, Chronic Diarrhoea,*

# Creepers

*Foul Breath, Incontinence* (Josh shuddered when he read that one), *Stinking Armpits, Brown Stumpy Teeth, Green Pus-Filled Spots, Yellow Pus-Filled Spots, Huge Whiteheads* and, finally, *Triple Combination Spots*.

"That's it." He stopped. *"The Triple Combination –* that's what he's given me!"

Glancing further up, Josh saw a large notice above the shelves that read AFFLICTIONS & AILMENTS. Looking to the other side of the room, he saw that the notice above those shelves read CURES & REMEDIES. The jars on the top shelf there were also labelled. *Shiny, Well-Conditioned Hair, Healthy Bowel Movements, Sweet Smelling Breath, Even White Teeth, Clear Perfect Skin.* He stopped reading and did a double take. *Clear Perfect Skin –* a dream come true! He'd check it out later – for now, though, he had to concentrate on whatever else he was able to find in the room.

Going back to the AFFLICTIONS & AILMENTS side, he began to read the labels on the jars that lined the second shelf. *Measles, Mumps, Chickenpox, Whooping Cough* and so on.

"Bit more serious" Josh thought, shaking his head. "This Dr Blair must really be a bit of a nutcase. He must have discovered, somehow, a way of 'bottling' these illnesses and then spent the rest of the time getting them into children's bodies. What a sicko!"

Looking at the corresponding shelf on the CURES & REMEDIES side of the room, he saw syringes lying beside jars that simply had the name of the illness printed on the label, with the word "vaccine" added below. More than a little anxious now, Josh was almost afraid to look at the third shelf.

He swallowed hard, and looked down. *Partial or Complete Paralysis* the first one read. Josh blanched. *Loss of Sight* said the second. Josh could feel the skin start to prickle on the back of his neck. He looked at the third. *Terminal Illness*. He knew, almost before he turned, what he would see when he looked at the corresponding right hand shelf. It was completely empty.

He heard a creaking noise. The doctor had come back and was about to catch Josh red-handed snooping about in his dispensary! He tried to flatten himself against the wall, attempting to calm down his breathing.

"Josh?" he heard. "Josh, are you in there?"

Josh exhaled deeply with relief. It was Simon – thank goodness for that.

"In here, Simon, but prepare yourself for a real shock. This guy's a real Dr Death, I'm not joking – you'll never believe what I've just found."

# Creepers

Simon came into the dispensary, closely followed by Kevin and Charlie. Josh indicated the notices above each wall of shelves and left the boys to read what was in each jar while he went back into the doctor's surgery to sit quietly at the desk. Simon was the first to join him, having seen all he needed to in the Chamber of Horrors next door. Neither boy spoke, waiting instead for their two friends to absorb everything they had just seen. Kevin and Charlie joined them fairly soon.

"Knew the guy was a weirdo," said Josh. "But I didn't expect to find all this stuff." Visibly shocked, his three friends could only nod. "How could anyone do such terrible things? I mean, what does he do – inject illnesses into young children then pretend to be concerned when they get really sick? And does he cure them right at the last minute or does he . . . does he simply . . ." Josh couldn't finish the sentence. It was just too awful to contemplate. The boys sat in silence, each with their own separate thoughts. "Anyone got any ideas, then?" asked Charlie. "What are we going to do?"

Standing up and pushing back his chair, Josh got to his feet. "I know," he announced, looking determined. "We're going to swap the labels, that's what we're going to do. We're going to swap over the labels so that next time Dr Death prescribes *Triple Combination Spots* for someone he'll really be giving them *Clear Skin*. And next time he prescribes *Extremely Large and Flaky Dandruff*, he'll really be prescribing *Shiny, Well Conditioned Hair*. Come on guys, we'd better get to work, we've got a lot to do."

"But Josh – what about the third shelf? We don't have any jars to swap with," said Charlie.

"I know, I already thought of that. One of us has to go to the supermarket, it should still be open (he checked his watch) and buy some bottles of food coloring. We'll simply empty out the contents of the jars then mix the food coloring with water and do a re-fill job. We'll just have to be really careful and make sure the doctor doesn't suspect."

Simon volunteered to go get the food coloring and, as he left by the window, checking carefully to make sure no-one saw him leave, his friends had already got down to work. They carried out the task quietly, gently removing each label and affixing it to its new home.

Before their job was complete, Josh took four small tubs and placed them carefully on the desk. Taking the larger container marked *Clear Perfect Skin*, he poured just enough to fill the first of the tubs. He replaced the large container on the shelf, then took the one marked *Sweet Smelling Breath* and filled a tub with that, too. He repeated the process twice more, filling the two remaining tubs with cures for Charlie and Kevin. He screwed the lids on all four tubs, marking each with details of its contents, and put them in a bag.

When Simon returned, most of the re-labeling was complete, and the boys then started to pour out the contents of the jars from the third shelf. They carefully mixed the food coloring with some water, ensuring it was just the right shade before pouring it into the appropriate jars. Eventually, everything returned to its proper place, the boys stood back and surveyed their handiwork.

"Well done, boys, good job. We'll see just how much damage Dr Death can do now!"

Leaving the dispensary, Josh once again pressed the button on the desk and closed the doors. He put his file in its rightful position in the filing cabinet, then, lifting the bag containing the stolen cures, he and his three friends opened the window and crept out into the night.

It was darker now, and the boys had to stop under a lamp post, using its light to see the words hastily scribbled on the tops of the tubs.

"There you go, guys. I'd start taking that as soon

as I got home if I were you. I know I will be. In fact I think I'll have two teaspoons before I go to bed," said Josh.

"I think I might drink the whole tub tonight" said Simon. "Anything, anything to get rid of this odor."

Charlie and Kevin smiled and took their tubs from Josh.

"What do you think will happen," asked Kevin, "when he starts to notice that people aren't getting sick any more?"

Josh shrugged. "Who knows? It may be that we're going to have to take this whole thing further at a later stage, but for now I think we did well."

"Yaah, you're right, Josh," agreed Charlie. "Let's go home and get some sleep – I'm bushed – and we'll get together in the morning to see how our cures are progressing."

Congratulating themselves, then, on what they had been able to do, though still anxious to know the final outcome, the weary boys said goodnight and began to make their way home.

# Chapter 9:

# Back to Normality

"You see, what did I tell you," said Josh's mom as he came bounding downstairs next morning for breakfast. "Worse before better – your Gran and Dr Blair were both right after all."

Josh grinned, pausing again to admire himself in the mirror. His skin, though not yet completely clear, looked three quarters of the way to being cured. He still had a few red pimples on his forehead but, apart from that, he both looked and felt great.

Meeting up with the boys later that morning en route to school, he found that they too were well on their way back to normality.

"Best medicine the doctor's ever prescribed," announced Charlie.

A few hours before, Dr Blair had arrived in his surgery. He always went there early in the morning, well before his receptionist and patients, and went straight to the dispensary. After locking the door of the surgery, he removed several of the jars from the dispensary, carefully placing them in an orderly row on his desk. Then, taking a small spoon from his drawer, he unscrewed the lid of the first jar and swallowed a spoonful. He did the same with the second jar and repeated the process all the way down the line. If the boys could have seen him now, they would have laughed out loud at the sight of the good doctor readily swallowing his ailments and afflictions.

# Chapter 10:

# Doctor Yeuch!

It was English, the last lesson on a Friday afternoon. A month had passed since the events that took place in the surgery, and all four boys were completely cured. The sun was streaming in the classroom window as the boys listened to their teacher sum up the final scene from *Macbeth*. Simon pushed a note towards Josh.

"Where are you going tonight?" Josh smiled before writing "Meeting Karen at 7 and going to the movies – will you and Cindy be there?"

Before Simon had time to scribble his reply, the final bell rang and both boys grabbed books and bags before running happily out of the classroom and into the summer sunshine.

The receptionist took another sip of her coffee, and turned the pages of her newspaper to the "Situations Vacant" pages. She was startled by her buzzer. She sighed.

"Yes, Dr Blair?"

"Would you bring my coffee?" he rasped.

# Creepers

"Certainly, doctor."

She got up from her chair and walked into the kitchen. She put some coffee and cookies on a tray and walked towards the doctor's room. She always dreaded this part. Taking a deep breath, she knocked twice on the door, turned the handle and went in. The stench hit her as soon as she opened the door. The doctor, seated behind his desk, was barely recognisable as the smooth sophisticated Dr Blair she had originally come to work for. The man seated behind the desk was now completely bald, his eyes dull and lifeless and his once white and even teeth now reduced to brown, rotting stumps. He seemed to have shrunk in size, and appeared much thinner than he had done before. "Probably due to his frequent visits to the bathroom," the receptionist thought as she placed his coffee before him. "The poor man seems to suffer from chronic bouts of diarrhoea."

He muttered his thanks and she gratefully left the room. She'd really have to find another job soon, she thought as she walked slowly back to reception through the deserted waiting room. There hadn't been a patient in here for weeks now, and who could blame them? The change in the doctor in such a short space of time was really quite unbelievable.

# Doctor Death

He looked awful, he smelled awful, and he was so gruff in his manner that he frightened people away. She sat down and started to type. "Dear Sirs, I am writing in response to your recent advertisement...'

Dr Blair pressed the button on his desk and slowly made his way into his dispensary. He unscrewed the jar labelled *Shiny, Well Conditioned Hair* and greedily swallowed a large teaspoonful. He stopped to scratch his face, his dirty jagged nails accidentally catching the head of a spot, causing green pus to spurt from it and run down the side of his face to drip onto his collar. Lifting the jar labelled *Healthy Bowel Movements,* he wondered aloud.

"Maybe I'll have two teaspoonfuls today – maybe that would help..."

# Chapter 11:

# Return of the Doctor

Dr Blair was back at work after recovering from what he thought was a severe tummy bug. But, what ever could have brought it on?

He hadn't eaten anything dodgy. He hadn't seen any patients with this type of thing. He wondered over to his secret cupboard. Perhaps his potions had "gone off"?

He studied them. Scratched his chin. Mmm. What's this? He held a bottle up to the light. It looked murky and vile.

But then again, that's what it was meant to look like.

Wait a minute! There is a smudge on the label! Now, Dr Blair always wore special gloves when putting anything into these bottles, for obvious reasons. So, who had been tampering here!

Okay, he thought. So Josh, Simon and the rest are a bit brighter than I gave them credit for. Instead of being scared or angry, he smiled actually relishing the challenge.

# Creepers

"So," he thought, "these guys wanna play, do they?"

With that, he set about working out various formulas for new potions. He'd done a lot of this lately in order to get rid of the ailments that he now understood had been caused by Josh and his pals swapping labels and bottles.

"Ingenious," he muttered to himself, impressed by their cunning. Who knows, maybe they'd be working for him one day.

"Ah ha!"

He'd got it! The new potion!

He looked at all his workings on his jotter, amazed at his own cleverness.

"I am more than a match for these interfering, snotty-nosed kids! Who do they think they are dealing with?"

But he was not going to make the obvious error of giving them the potion. No. They'd be expecting that. Why, they may even have antidotes worked out. After all, they had rummaged through his secret stuff, so who knew that they knew? "

So, young Josh is on yet another date next week is he?" thought Dr Blair, remembering a conversation he had had with Josh's mom.

"You know what I wonder? I wonder if his date is

pretty. In fact I wonder if she would like to feel extra special for tonight. A date's a date and a girl has to feel her best, especially now that Josh's acne seems to have cleared up.

"What about this new line of 'perfume' I have developed?" thought the evil Doctor. "I bet she'd love that."

He made a mental note to ensure that Karen's mom had reason to call in. He made efforts to find the number. He gave it to his receptionist and instructed her to call Karen Summer's mom and others in that street and say that the nurse was doing a spot health check on families in the area due to all the strange bugs that seemed to be going around.

Sure enough, the gullible mums all dutifully brought their families along. It helped that he was once again considered the best looking doctor in town, now that he'd recovered his looks!

"Ah, Mrs Summers. Lovely to see you. I hope this spot check has not inconvenienced you too much but, I feel we should be trying to get to the bottom of all these outbreaks of horrible and embarrassing illnesses that seem to have plagued us."

"Yes, Doctor, I agree", said Mrs Summers.

"And you know what? The strange thing is that until you arrived, we had no problems of that nature at all. Oops. Sorry Doctor, that did not come out at all right, did it?"

"No offence taken, Mrs Summers. Now, let me check a couple of things. Has your Karen been a bit moody lately?"

"No. Not at all."

"I see. Just as I thought. See, the thing is Mrs Summers, if a girl her age is not moody, then something must be wrong, don't you agree?" His smile was engulfing. Mrs Summers uttered words that made no sense to her at all, like,

"Yes Doctor. You are right. I see what you mean." Well, what harm could it do to agree with a doctor?

"So, Mrs Summers, we recommend a new aromatherapy treatment that might do the trick. It's like a perfume – but natural. As a free trial, I am giving some away. Why not trial it for me?

"Here's one bottle for you," (he passed over a harmless substance that would smell vaguely pleasant), "and here is one for Karen" (and he passed a bottle that looked the same and, at first, would smell the same. That's where the similarity ended though).

"Why thank you Doctor. That's very kind. Karen has a date soon and so she will be very grateful indeed!"

# Doctor Death

Not for long, thought Dr Blair. Not that he cared. After he had his revenge on Josh, he would be gone forever. And if the town thought it had already suffered a mini-plague, then it had not seen anything yet.

# Chapter 12:

# Josh's Date

Josh waited for Karen at the ice cream café. This would be their third date and their first on their own without Simon and Cindy. Josh had been working on his best lines all day. Now, for the first time, he was a little nervous about the date.

"I hope I don't make an ass of myself," he thought as he checked his reflection in the window. Still, at least there were no spots to think of. Thank goodness Dr Blair had leaned his lesson and was behaving himself. Ah, here comes Karen now.

Josh's inner voice began to talk. Okay. Play it cool. I am the guy. It's up to me to keep this great thing we have going with excellent one-liners, and entertaining anecdotes. But what if they all run out before we finish our chocolate ice cream! Panic! Cool? Cool, you said. That's right. You said cool. Not flustered, or worried, or anxious, but cool, smooth, relaxed. Got that? Good.

Josh continued to chatter to himself in his head as he watched his dream girl approach.

# Creepers

"Hey!" he said, playing it cool.

"Hey you too!" she replied.

In they went. Josh thought he'd just caught a whiff of something unpleasant. The door closed behind them and they sat down and ordered the chocolate ice cream that had been on their minds most of the day. Summer was really great.

But, still, that whiff. Oh God, no! Josh's inner voice stared panicking in his head. 'Cool' we said! Not 'let's stand on dog dirt' cool – just 'actual' cool. No dog dirt needed!

Josh almost replied to his inner self out loud but stopped just in time. But the inner turmoil over the dog dirt on the shoe continued. Why, what else could it be? It must be dog dirt!

"Well?" said Karen, smiling.

With sweat breaking out on his brow, Josh was increasingly distracted by his own stupidity. Why couldn't he have watched where he was going! Tonight of all nights!

"Well, what?" he replied, eventually.

"Well, what do you think of my new perfume?"

Her perfume. Her perfume! How on earth could she talk about her perfume when the only aroma swirling around them was that of the dog dirt he'd obviously stood on! Maybe she had a summer cold or something. How else could she not smell it? Still, he wasn't going to bring it to her attention.

"Oh, the perfume? Oh, that. It's very nice."

"Really? I'm so glad. I was getting funny looks on the bus on the way over here. I was sure people didn't like it. Either that or something else was bothering them. Anyway, you like it. And that's the main thing. Here, you try some."

Karen took a bottle out of her bag and thrust it up to Josh's nose. It was the perfume bottle. She took the top off and offered it to him to sniff it. But Josh had to turn away – it was revolting! It was like dog dirt except it was worse than that! Elephant dirt! He felt sick. And he immediately realised that it was Karen's "perfume" that was stinking the place out! But how could she not know! Other people in the café were now looking round. Some were holding their noses. A lady was holding her baby's nose as it squealed with horror at the smell! And here was Karen, the girl of his dreams, sitting there. Her smile had gone. She looked like she wanted to know what was wrong with her "perfume". And here was Josh, cool dude Josh, who was going to have to tell the girl of his dreams that she smelt like a skunk. Yeah, that's cool, Josh.

Josh broke the news, feeling that she'd understand

and maybe even thank him. Except that she did not wait around to thank him. She just tipped over her chair as she left. Josh was left sitting there on his own. But the smell had gone. People breathed again.

But poor Karen! Josh couldn't work it out. Why was she the only person who could not smell that smell from her perfume?

# Chapter 13:

# The Doctor Calls

Just then, Dr Blair walked in.

"My, it's a lovely night, folks, isn't it?"

The assembled folks still revered Dr Blair the way some might revere a priest. There was almost a collective tipping of the hat to him.

Josh felt sick. Why was he here? He'd lain low since his ailments, but now here he was, full of happiness. And poor Karen was running back to the bus stop, crying. And Josh was sitting here, confused. This was not fair at all. Just then, Dr Blair lent over to Josh as he passed his table.

"Having a nice night, Josh?" he growled.

"No."

"Good! Remember, don't pick fights with guys who are bigger than you, small fry!"

And then he went about his hellos, and chatted with the customers.

Josh looked up and saw the good doctor sitting with a pair of mums, and watched them all laughing. He recognised one of the women as Cindy's mom.

# Creepers

They were joking around and then Cindy's mom produced a bottle, not unlike the one Karen had just shown him. The doctor began to frown. In fact, he could clearly be heard saying, "Put that away, woman!" Cindy's mom looked upset. After all, who was she to upset this great man? "I'm sorry, doctor, I was just so grateful for the perfume you gave me and Cindy. In fact Cindy is wearing hers tonight on a date with Simon.

Josh's mind just clicked! So, if the perfume bottle Karen showed me was given to her by that creep, then mystery solved!

He stood up quickly and went to run out of the café before Dr Blair realised that he was on to him. But, the café owner shouted over, "Hey, Josh! You are not leaving without paying are you? Settle your bill please!"

Dr Blair's mind also clicked. He suddenly knew why Josh was in a rush. And he was wondering how to stop him without looking strange. Josh threw down the money and rushed to leave, but heard Dr Blair's voice shout,

"Hey, Josh. How are you tonight?"

Josh's patience was over with this guy. And he wanted to get to his girl to explain that she had done nothing wrong.

# Doctor Death

"I said, how are you doing?" repeated Dr Blair.

"You already know how I am doing!" cried Josh across the café.

Customers sat up and a collective "ooooh" went through the place. The doctor sensed a showdown.

"Oh, I should know? I am a good doctor but I am not a mind-reader, boy!"

The place laughed, and murmurs of "Oh yes he is a good doctor" could be heard.

"But you are a chemist, I see!"

"What?"

"A chemist. You know, someone who..."

"I know what a chemist is, sonny. But in case you can't read, the sign above my door says 'Doctor' – not 'chemist'."

"Which door?" asked Josh.

"What do you mean 'which door'?"

"Oh, I though you might be referring to the secret door inside your office, not the one outside it. You know, the secret compartment?"

But Dr Blair was no mug. He'd been in this scenario many times. He'd outsmarted many kids in many towns and he wasn't going to let this soon-to-be-spotty-again kid expose him. Blair knew all the tricks.

"Ah yes, my secret compartment. Pray, tell. How

would you know about such a thing, even if it did exist? Which it doesn't."

Josh could see the trap the Doctor had just skilfully set but Josh just could not stop himself from falling into it.

"Because we saw it the night we broke into your place."

The collective "ooooh" in the café became louder!

This was as close to a courtroom drama as Dr Blair ever wanted to get to. So he really went for it.

"Ah, let me recap. You mean, that you went into my office when I wasn't there?"

"Yes," replied Josh, going red, suddenly realising he was now the bad guy in the eyes of the café crowd.

Just then the owner piped up:

"And the little thief tried to run out of here without paying too!"

Josh knew when it was time to quit. The good doctor had this jury in the palm of his hand. And Josh had to get out of there, regardless of how incriminating it might look. He had to find Karen. And then he'd have to hide. What a night this was turning out to be. Yeah, said the voice in his head, very cool.

Josh had to use a few of his best body-swerve

moves learned from school sports to get out of the café while dodging customers who thought it only right that they should try to stop him.

"Just you wait until your mother hears about this young man!" shouted one.

"Just wait until the police hear about this, young man!" shouted Blair, smiling. My, he'd played this one beautifully. Josh had a lot to learn about how to be a bad guy.

# Chapter 14:

# Karen Figures it Out

Josh was on the street. No sign of Karen at the bus stop. He asked a couple waiting for the bus if they'd seen a girl there earlier.

"Yeah, she was crying. She wondered off when we got here. I shouted that the bus was just a few minutes away, but she still walked off", said the lady.

"Which way?"

Josh ran down the way the lady pointed. A few minutes later, the same lady saw a man running up to her, breathless. "Which way?" he gasped and the lady pointed in the same direction.

Josh eventually caught up with Karen. She was sitting on a park bench. She was not crying now but it was obvious that she had been. Her eyes were red. But at least she did not smell like before. He noted the perfume bottle in the bin beside the chair.

"I'm sorry, Josh."

"What for? It wasn't your fault. In fact, it was mine." He sat down beside her, unaware that, behind him, a man was following him as best he could, but as he was unfit, he was slow in catching up.

"How do you mean, 'your fault'?"

"Look, you are not going to believe me. But see that Dr Blair?

He deliberately gave you that stinking perfume so that our date would be bad. See, it ain't you he hates. It's me."

Karen looked at him with a remarkable lack of surprise.

"That creep. My mom gushes every time his name is mentioned. He's just a phoney though."

"You, you know? How do you know?"

"I figured it out looking at the perfume. And then started thinking about all the stuff people had wrong with them. They were fine before they went to the doctor. Then they were ill. I never smelled like dog dirt before, and then he gave me perfume and suddenly I smelled revolting. It's not a mystery is it? But the thing is, the grown ups will never believe us."

"I know. In fact, thanks to him, I am now on the town's most-wanted list. I'd be surprised if I was not being chased by a lynch mob. Look, until the town wises up, which it may never do, we just have to keep each other strong – you, me, the guys, Cindy. In the meantime, whereabouts in the proceedings had we got to on that date?"

"Well, I think you were thinking about putting your arm around me."

"Was I? My, that would have been brave of me. Were we at that bit already? Well, let's see if we can get back to that."

Karen looked over Josh's shoulder and said, "We might do, except I think that might be your lynch mob arriving!"

And with that they both stood up to run. But it was not a mob, it was only one man. It was the man who had followed Josh to the bus stop and had then been pointed in his direction by the lady there. Josh immediately thought it might be Dr Blair, chasing him with some obscene potion or something. But it wasn't Dr Blair. Perhaps it was one of the outraged café customers, wanting to capture Josh to take him to his mom, and expose him as someone who had burgled the doctor's office. Josh stood there, determined to face whatever happened next with dignity. He'd have his day in court, soon. That's right, said the inner voice, this time without sarcasm, cool, very cool.

The man saw them and broke into a run again until he caught up with them.

"Wait!"

But Josh was waiting. He said, "Yeah? What do you want?"

The man ran up to Josh and put his hand out towards his. "Put it there, lad, put it there!" The man obviously wanted to shake Josh's hand. Josh obliged.

"What's going on?"

"I was in the café. Tonight they'll hate you, but in the morning, you'll be a hero!"

"I don't understand!"

"No, nor did we. Until your scene in the café! I am sorry," wheezed the breathless man, "let me introduce myself. I am Inspector Crook, police. We've been on this guy's trail for years. But he keeps changing his appearance, his identity, everything. And we only get to know when it's too late, like when he's moved to some new town, leaving a trail of devastation behind him. We've been getting closer and closer and tonight we heard what we needed to hear in the café."

"What was that?" asked a puzzled Josh

"The secret compartment. Usually, his surgeries burn down just before he leaves town. But here we are, just before he planned to leave, and we have a witness to the fact that there is a secret compartment in his surgery. You. And all we need to do is get you to take us there. And then we'll expose him. My colleagues have arrested him back at the café. They had to fight their way out with him, as the customers all love him!"

"Tell us about it!" said both Karen and Josh.

"Anyway, Josh, I need you to come and show us where the Doctor's evil store is."

# Chapter 15:

# The Last Laugh

An hour later, Josh, Inspector Crook and two of his colleagues, were in the secret compartment. But it was empty!

"He must have known someone was on to him!" cried the inspector.

Just then, an officer arrived with much needed coffee for the detectives.

"Oh, thanks very much!"

And they all gulped down their coffee. Then something very strange happened. Inspector Crook put his coffee down and said to the others, who were still drinking theirs, "Okay guys, let's go."

With that, they finished their coffee and sauntered off. Josh and Karen looked at each other, amazed! They ran after the police.

"Where are you going?"

"What?" replied Crook, adding:

"Hey, what you kids doing up so late anyway. Go on. Off home with you!"

Josh and Karen looked at each other. And then

both said to each other, "THE COFFEE!"

They ran back to the doctor's office and found just the empty cups, no coffee left. They picked up the cups and they did not smell of coffee at all! They looked at each other again.

"Did you get a look at that officer?

You know, the one that brought the coffee?" asked Josh.

Karen, looking out the window, said:

"No, but there he is getting into that police car!" They ran out to see the car starting up. Josh's mind clicked like it had done in the café. He knocked on the driver's window. The car was full. Crook and the others were inside. The officer was driving.

"Stop!" cried Josh.

The car stopped like Josh had wanted it to, only now that it had, he wasn't so sure this was a good thing any more. The driver's window slid down. The officer looked out at them. He smiled.

"Remind you of anyone?" he asked wickedly.

"Blair!" cried Josh.

"Officer Blair to you! Now, you kids, listen good. I am going to cut you a little slack here. I have put a potion in the town's drinking water. Don't panic – it's a good potion. It will make everyone forget all this unpleasantness. Now ain't that a good thing?"

# Doctor Death

A voice from the back seat asked what the hold up was. It was Inspector Crook. Officer Blair just looked at Josh and Karen while shouting into the back of the car:

"Drink up all your coffee, boys, drink it all up, now." He smiled at them.

"See, you young lovebirds, I took pity on your sad and stupid town. I always do. Who gets hurt, huh? No one. Not really. It's just my way of staying awake in a boring world. You guys gave me a run for my money though. I don't mind telling you, I felt excited. Like I was going to get caught. I have not felt that for years! So my little thank you is that no one will remember, and you can all go back to being boring.

Now, Josh, don't tell me you were not just a little excited by pitting your wits against mine."

Josh was silent. The doctor was wrong. At least, Josh hoped he was. Karen did too. Then Josh piped up, "So, the whole town forgets you. The dumb cops here have already forgotten you, thanks to your specially brewed coffee I presume. However, you are forgetting one little thing."

"Oh yeah", sighed Blair, already bored, as he already knew the rest off this conversation backwards. He'd had this chat with the Joshes and

# Creepers

Karens of the world many times in many towns, usually right about now, just before he fired off into the sunset, laughing at the fools left behind in his rear view mirror one more time.

"Yeah! Karen and I will remember everything. And we have not had any coffee, and we won't drink water from this town, we'll tell everyone what you have just confessed to! We have had none of your forgetting potions!"

The car window started to move upwards. Blair looked at them one last time.

"Did you guys enjoy that chocolate ice cream at the café? Well, that one was on me." He smiled and winked as the window slid all the way up and the car roared away with its siren sounding and its lights flashing, leaving Josh and Karen feeling woosy, tired, forgetful.

# BEGGAR BOY

Tommy and his mum move to a new house and all
their neighbours seem to be better off than them.
The other kids from the area take great pleasure in
picking on Tommy and always remind him how
poor he and his Mum are. Tommy then gets help
from a curious lad that seems to appear when he
needs a friend. In fact, with his new friend, he takes
revenge on the snobbish kids around him.
But where did this mysterious friend come from?
And why is he helping Tommy?

# THE PIANO

The Houston family appear to have found a great bargain when they buy a beautiful piano for a really low price. However, the piano seems to have a mind of its own. In fact, no matter what tune people try to play on it, the piano wants to play its own haunting music.
What is the piano trying to tell the world?
And have the Houstons got more than they bargained for?

# THE SCARECROW

In the countryside, people often become attached to the land that they are born on – but a scarecrow? Mysterious happenings on the Davis land make young David too curious for his own good. But the more he investigates, the more he wishes that he'd kept his mouth shut. And so does the scarecrow!

# GHOST WRITER

Charlie is a schoolboy with a talent for writing but even he cannot remember writing all the words that appear in his note book. There seems to be a story being told on the pages of his note book but who is doing the telling? Charlie's headmaster is showing just a little too much interest in the note book and does not seem very happy with Charlie. Ever been scared of your headmaster?
I mean REALLY scared!

# THE
# WISHING WELL

Tom finds solace from the world when he
stumbles across a disused well near his home. In
fact, whatever he wishes for comes true as long as
he asks for it at the well. In this well, there is a spirit
granting his wishes, but what will this ghost
want in return?
And what happens when Tom hesitates in
helping the spirit of the wishing well?

# BLOOD ON TAP

Bill Todd is delighted to have found a new house for his family. It's cheap, in a good neighborhood and it will provide the much-needed space for his growing family. His wife and his young children – Alex, Beth, Gary and Karen – are not so sure.

The house looks sinister and feels even more creepy. They all have a very bad feeling about it, but Mr Todd will not change his mind. Number 13 Blackday Avenue is just what it appears to be, and very soon they encounter something that makes them wish they had never moved.

# THE GHOSTLY SOLDIER

Angus and Isobel love to hear the stories about heroic Scottish warriors. They visit the site where the Battle of Culloden was fought and Angus romanticizes the events, wishing that he could have been there to help fight the Redcoats. His opinion changes when an explosion in their garden unleashes the spirits of the English and Scottish soldiers who must fight the battle again and again. The children must return the spirits to where they belong.
But how?

# Edgar Escapes

After bringing many other ghostly and despicable tales to your notice I decided that I must tell my own story. Confronted with this demand for knowledge, I felt it was only correct that I should submit my story to you. Dear reader, I would not be anything without your attention. Dear reader, I will reveal the person behind the stories, where I am from, just how I tell my tales from behind the grave and the deadly purpose I have. Now, I ask you to read on – if you dare!

# SOUL HARVEST

The Grimaldis, a creepy new family who have a bad attitude and who dress in black move into Billy and Alice's neighborhood. Very soon afterwards their mom and dad and all the other neighbours start to act very strangely – as if they have suddenly become wicked. The children, and their friends Ricky and Alex, are soon the only normal ones left in a neighborhood of thieves, bullies and thugs. The entire village, headed by the Grimaldis, are soon trying to find the four children and capture their souls to make the imminent "harvest" complete!

# MIRROR MIRROR

The Johnstone family buy an old mirror. Soon, the children of the household think they can see an image of a girl trapped inside it. She is dressed in strange clothes and seems to be trying to communicate with the children.
What is the mysterious story of the girl?
And why is she trapped in the mirror?

# Happy Halloween

Samantha, James and Mandy are brother and sisters.
Their parents decide to take a break in a quiet village
the weekend of Halloween. The children are rather
concerned that staying in a boring village is going to
spoil their trick-or-treating. Halloween is certainly
going to be very different to usual
– but it will be far from boring!
Samantha discovers an old spell book and that she
alone is capable of harnessing its dangerous pow-
ers. She is soon drawn into a sinister and terrifying
world of wizards and witches and must escape or
lose her life and risk the safety of the normal world.